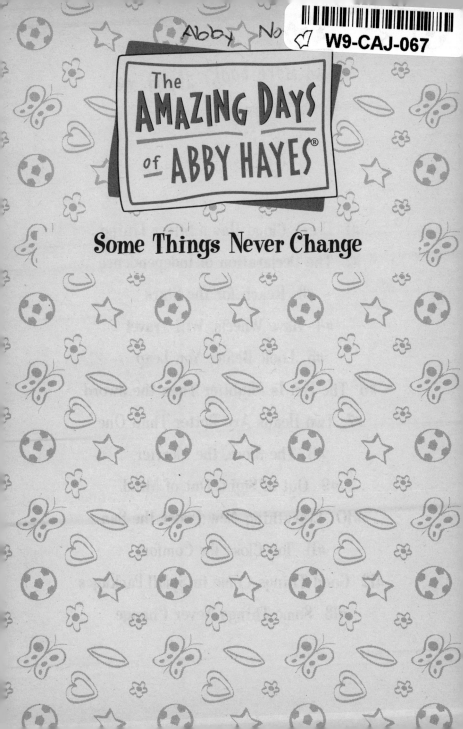

Abby No

The AMAZING DAYS of ABBY HAYES®

Some Things Never Change

Read more books about me!

The AMAZING DAYS of ABBY HAYES®

Some Things Never Change

ANNE MAZER

AN
APPLE
PAPERBACK

SCHOLASTIC INC.
New York Toronto London Auckland Sydney
Mexico City New Delhi Hong Kong Buenos Aires

No part of this publication may be reproduced in whole or in part, or stored in a retrieval system, or transmitted in any form or by any means, electronic, mechanical, photocopying, recording, or otherwise, without written permission of the publisher. For information regarding permission, write to Scholastic Inc., Attention: Permissions Department, 557 Broadway, New York, NY 10012.

ISBN 0-439-48281-X

12 11 10 9 8 7 6 5 4 3   4 5 6 7 8 9/0

Printed in the U.S.A.   40

First printing, April 2004

To Elaine Markson

Chapter 1

> **Tuesday**
>
> "He who sings frightens away his ills."
>
> —Cervantes
>
> **Nights at the Opera Calendar**

<u>She</u> who sings frightens away her class-mates?

In a few minutes, Brianna will sing for our class. She is "showcasing her talent," as she explained to us.

Ms. Kantor gave us an assignment to do oral reports on our hobbies. Earlier today, I read a story I wrote. It's called "In the Sandbox." The main characters are two five-year-olds. Everyone laughed a lot when I read it.

Yesterday, Hannah gave a report on tropical fish. She brought in the tropical fish mobile that usually hangs in her bedroom.

Ms. Kantor let her do her report a day early because Hannah has a doctor's appointment this morning.

This morning, Bethany talked about gymnastics and did a few cartwheels in front of the class. Zach and Tyler each did a report on computer games. Now it's Brianna's turn.

Brianna is the best-dressed girl in the fifth grade. Today she is wearing a frilly white blouse and shiny blue satin capri pants. Her lips are colorful — is it tinted lip gloss or actual lipstick? Brianna has tiny gold earrings, too!

Some of us have mothers who won't let us get our ears pierced until seventh grade! That's two years from now! <u>I can't wait that long!</u>

Brianna just got up in front of the room.

The Brianna Performance

1. She closes her eyes.
2. She sighs deeply.
3. She puts her hand over her heart.

The Audience Wonders

1. Is she going to sleep?
2. Is she ill?
3. Is she going to faint or scream?

Now she's flinging her arms out and opening her mouth.

I think she's going to sing.

Brianna's Songs

1. "I've Gotta Be Me"
2. "My Way"
3. "Unforgettable"

Brianna _is_ unforgettable. She will go down in the <u>Hayes Book of World Records</u> as Sappiest Soprano on the Best of the Boast page.

Brianna Takes a Bow

"Thank you, thank you. What a pleasure
it is to be here today. I know you're all
dying to hear more. I'll be singing at City
Theater on Saturday night. Thank you!"
(Blows kisses.) "I'll also be reciting a poem
called 'Song of Myself.'"

Brianna Makes a Public Service Announcement

"There are only a few tickets left
for my Saturday night performance.
They're going fast! Get yours now."
Do people actually pay to
see Brianna?

"Thank you, Brianna," Ms. Kantor, the fifth-grade
teacher, said. "What a privilege it is to have so many
talented students in our class."

Brianna smirked. "I'm the *most* talented."

"*I* won the lead for the school play," Natalie muttered. She had beaten out Brianna for the starring
role in *Peter Pan*. Natalie was one of Abby's good
friends. Her short hair was rumpled and messy. She

wore jeans, sneakers, and a striped T-shirt.

Brianna pretended she hadn't heard. She waved like a movie star and acknowledged her fans.

"I'm the *only* fifth-grader in the *county* who performs at City Theater," she said.

"And she'll never let us forget it, either," Natalie said to Abby.

Ms. Kantor clapped her hands for attention. "While we're on the subject of talent . . . would anyone be interested in participating in a talent show?"

Almost twenty hands rocketed into the air.

"Me!" Natalie cried.

"I'll perform," Brianna said. "Of course."

Ms. Kantor continued, "Mrs. McMillan and I have decided to collaborate on a talent show for the two fifth grades. Everyone can participate."

"Everyone?" Brianna's lip curled scornfully.

"Everyone," Ms. Kantor repeated. "If you have an act, we want to see it. All kinds of talent are welcome. Singing, dancing, acting, playing musical instruments, reciting . . ."

"Burping?" Mason asked.

"No, Mason," Ms. Kantor said. "There *are* limits."

"Can I do gymnastics in the talent show?" Bethany

asked. She moved her hands and feet as if she were about to launch into another cartwheel.

"Yes," Ms. Kantor said. She glanced at the clock. "Let's take a few minutes right now to talk about our ideas."

"I'm going to act out a scene from one of my favorite fantasy novels!" Natalie declared.

"That sounds great!" Bethany said.

Natalie smiled. "You can be part of it."

"Gymnastics *and* acting?" Abby commented. "I'd get double stage fright."

Bethany looked worried. "Do you think it's too much?"

"We can combine the two. I'll work a gymnastics part into the scene," Natalie said to Bethany. "You'll have magical somersault powers."

Bethany's eyes lit up. "Will you put in a part for Blondie, too?" she asked Natalie. Blondie was Bethany's beloved hamster.

"I've never seen a hamster in a fantasy novel," Natalie said. "But why not?"

"What about you, Abby? Do you want to join us?" Bethany asked.

Abby shook her head. "I'd rather watch the talent show than be in it."

"You can't mean that," Brianna said. "It's *always* better to be onstage."

"Remember when you rewrote *Peter Pan*?" Natalie reminded Abby. "That was *great*."

The creative writing teacher, Ms. Bunder, had given Abby the job of updating the *Peter Pan* script. Everyone had loved what she did with it.

"That was different," Abby said slowly. "Other people acted out my words. I didn't have to be onstage — except to narrate. And that was just reading."

"Didn't you try out for a few parts?" Bethany asked.

"Yeah." Abby shrugged. "But that was then. This is now."

"You'll miss out on a *lot* of fun," Natalie warned.

"Are you waiting for Hannah to decide?" Bethany asked. "Is that why you don't want to join us?"

Hannah and Abby had become good friends over the summer when Hannah had gone on a camping trip with the Hayes family. Then Hannah's family had moved into Abby's neighborhood. Now she was in Ms. Kantor's class.

"Not really," Abby said. She just didn't want to be

in the talent show. Not even with Hannah, who was practically her best friend.

"Too bad Hannah had an appointment this morning and had to miss this," Bethany commented.

"Hannah will be in the talent show," Natalie predicted. "She's so *not* shy. I can't imagine her saying no."

"She'll talk you into it," Bethany said to Abby. "Just wait. She'll come up with a great idea."

Abby smiled. Hannah was known for her great ideas. "Maybe," she said. "Or maybe not."

Chapter 2

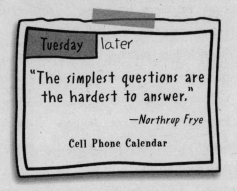

Tuesday later

"The simplest questions are the hardest to answer."

—Northrup Frye

Cell Phone Calendar

<u>Simple Questions That Are the Hardest to Answer</u>

1. Why don't I want to be in the talent show?
2. Why won't I join my friends in one of their acts?
3. Why can't I do <u>something</u>?
4. Why don't I at least read a poem?

These are some of the things that Natalie and Bethany and other classmates asked me.

Casey, who is in the other fifth-grade

class, asked me to do an act with him. Even though he's a boy, he's my friend. He's not computer-obsessed like Zach and  Tyler. He doesn't burp and act obnoxious like Mason. (Though Mason can be nice, too.) Casey likes a lot of the same things I do. He walks to school with Hannah and me every day.

"Let's think of something to do together," Casey said to me at recess. "It'll be great!"

When I refused, he also wanted to know why I didn't want to be in the talent show.

Answers

1. Because.
2. That's why.
3. I don't feel like it.
4. I don't want to.
5. It's the wrong phase of the moon.
6. I don't know.

Then Hannah came over to my house after school.

Natalie was right about her.

She <u>does</u> want to be in the talent show, and she has LOTS of ideas.

Hannah's Inventive Ideas

1. Dress like a clown and act silly.
2. Sing a song.
3. Put on a magic show.
4. Do a skit.
5. Rollerblade to music.

Hannah will get a mention for Totally Terrific Talent Show Ideas in the <u>Hayes Book of World Records</u>.

Hannah and I made popcorn and brought it up to my room. We sat on the floor with my cat, T-Jeff, curled up between us. Hannah told me all her exciting ideas. I had to tell her that I didn't want to do any of them.

"I'm sorry. I just don't want to," I said.

Hannah understood. "Maybe another time," she said.

"Maybe," I said.

She said she was sorry, too.

"There are a lot of kids who don't want to perform," Hannah said after a moment. "In Mrs. McMillan's class, there are only six kids who're going to be in the show."

"Like Casey," I said. I grabbed another handful of popcorn. Then I had my brainstorm.

"Casey!" I shouted, spewing a few stray kernels.

Hannah stared at me. "Casey?"

"Casey. Why don't you do something with Casey? He asked _me_ to do a skit with him. He'd be thrilled to do one with you." I waited for Hannah to jump up and down.

"I don't know . . ." she said slowly.

"He'd be a perfect partner!" I cried. "Can't you see it? You'd be great together!"

Hannah took some more popcorn. Then she looked at me. "Are you _sure_ it's okay?"

"It's okay," I said, scratching T-Jeff under his chin.

"You're my first choice. I want you to know that."

"I'd be relieved if you and Casey did a skit together," I told her. "Really."

She hugged me. "You're the greatest."

Hannah is the greatest. I'm so glad she's my friend. I wonder what she and Casey will do together. I bet it'll be funny.

After Hannah left to walk home, Abby went downstairs.

From the kitchen came the faint sounds of two arguing older sisters.

"Not again," Abby sighed. Sometimes it seemed as if all her twin sisters shared was a last name.

She didn't investigate. It was never wise to get between Eva and Isabel when they were fighting.

Abby headed back upstairs. As she reached the landing, the door to Alex's room flew open.

Alex, her younger brother, was wearing a wizard's hat, a long cape, and knee-high rubber boots.

"*What* are you doing, Alex?" Abby asked.

He ignored her question. "Abby!" he cried. "You got a letter!"

"From Grandma Emma?" she asked eagerly. Grandma Emma was her favorite relative. She sent Abby letters in handmade envelopes.

"Nope," Alex said. He smiled mysteriously, twirled his hat, and disappeared into his room.

When Abby entered her room, she saw the letter lying on her desk and knew instantly who had written it.

She stared at it for a moment but didn't touch it. Then the phone rang. Abby picked up the cordless phone in the hall and brought it into her room.

"Guess what?" Hannah cried.

"You won a trillion dollars," Abby joked. "You're going to have your own indoor swimming pool, Rollerblading rink, and movie theater."

"Better than that. I ran into Casey on the way home from your house."

"*That's* better than a trillion dollars?"

Hannah laughed. "He's going to join me in an act for the talent show!"

"Great," Abby said. "What are you going to do?"

"We don't know yet," Hannah said.

"Do something funny," Abby urged.

"Yeah," Hannah agreed. "So what's new with *you*?"

"Since five minutes ago?" Abby glanced at the

desk. "I got a letter," she said. "Guess who it's from?"

"Who?" Hannah said.

Abby paused dramatically. "Jessica."

"Your best friend who went to live with her dad?"

"*Former* best friend," Abby corrected.

Since she had moved away, Jessica was a different person than the one Abby had been friends with beginning with kindergarten. Now she was *Jessy*.

Jessica had liked science, especially astronomy. She wore baggy overalls and striped tops. She liked to pin smiley-face buttons on her clothing and backpack. Her room was always neat and organized. *Jessy* liked boys and parties. Abby didn't know how she dressed anymore, but she didn't think Jessy wore overalls or smiley-face buttons. She wondered if Jessy's room at her dad's house was neat.

"What did she say?" Hannah asked.

"I haven't opened it yet."

"Are you serious?"

"She never answers my e-mails," Abby said. "I haven't heard from her in months. I'm not that excited to hear from her."

"Aren't you curious?" Hannah said. "*I* am!"

Abby picked up the envelope. She held it in her hand for a moment and then quickly opened it. She glanced at its contents and tossed it back on the desk.

"*Tell* me!" Hannah cried impatiently on the other end of the line. "Read it! I mean, if you want to."

"Yeah. Okay." Abby picked up the letter and began to read. " 'Dear Abby, So hey, whatya doin'? How's good old Lancaster Elementary? Are you as tired of fifth grade as I am? I can't wait to go to middle school! Fifth grade is SOOOO boring! Danielle . . .' "

Abby broke off to explain. "That's her new stepsister. She's in fifth grade, too."

" '. . . Danielle and I are ice-skating in a competition on Saturday. We're wearing gold satin skirts and spaghetti-strap tops.' "

"The Jessica *I* knew wouldn't have been caught dead in a gold satin skirt or a spaghetti-strap top!" Abby exclaimed. She continued reading.

" 'And we expect to win first prize as we're the top-ranked skaters in our league. Next week I'm flying back to see my mother for spring vacation. Any parties happening? Any cute guys around? See ya soon!! Can't wait! *Jessy.*' "

"She's coming back?" Hannah cried. "Great! I'll get to meet her!"

"You want to meet her after *that* letter?"

"Sure. Why not?"

Abby folded up the letter and shoved it in a desk drawer. "I don't know why she wrote to me," she said slowly.

"Because," Hannah said, "she's your best friend."

"*Former* best friend," Abby repeated.

"Are you excited about seeing her?"

"I guess," said Abby. But she wasn't so sure.

Chapter 3

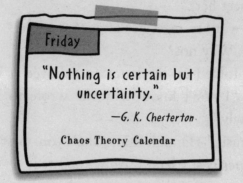

Friday

"Nothing is certain but uncertainty."

—G. K. Chesterton

Chaos Theory Calendar

What Is Certain

1. Jessica is coming back.
2. She will be here in a few days.
3. She is a different person than she used to be.

What Is Uncertain

1. Do we have anything in common?
2. Do we have anything to say to each other?
3. Will we even like each other?

Why does she have to visit now? A few months ago, I would have been thrilled to see her, even if she <u>had</u> turned into Jessy.

Now I don't miss her at all. Especially since Hannah and I are friends.

What ELSE Is Uncertain

1. Will Hannah and Jessica like each other?

2. Will Jessica think Casey is my boyfriend? (<u>I hope not!</u>)

3. Will she be surprised to find out that Natalie and Bethany are close friends?

4. Does she realize how much everything has changed?

5. I hope she doesn't expect me to spend all my time with <u>her</u>!!!

She will be here in a few days. I haven't told anyone she's coming back. Even Natalie doesn't know yet. Unless she knows and isn't saying anything to me.

P.S. I don't know if I'll remember to call her Jessy!! What if she gets mad when I call her Jessica??

"Is that stuff *really* mashed potatoes?" Natalie pointed to the stainless steel bins of food behind the glass counter of the cafeteria.

The fifth-graders were lined up with their trays to get their lunches.

"That's what it says on the chalkboard," Abby said. "Mashed potatoes."

"It looks like liquid glue," Zach said. "And it tastes like aged cardboard."

"Eeeeu," Bethany said. "Don't say that. I'm hungry!"

"I bet they squirt it out of metal tubes," Mason continued. "Maybe the leftovers get sent to factories for industrial use."

"Will you, like, *shut up?*" Victoria hissed. She turned to Brianna, who was her best friend. "Fifth-grade boys are so, like, totally immature."

"Fifth-grade girls are so, like, totally, totally, *totally* . . ." Mason mimicked.

Victoria glanced around the room to see whether any teachers were watching. Then she kicked him.

Mason only laughed. "Guess where meat loaf comes from? They grind the meat with plenty of grease . . ."

"Ignore him," Brianna said loudly.

"For once, I agree with Brianna," Abby muttered. She put a salad, a tuna sandwich, and a carton of chocolate milk on her tray. "Are you getting ice cream?" she asked Hannah.

"Not today," Hannah said.

"That pie looks good," Abby said.

Hannah put it on her tray. Then she picked up a turkey sub.

"Where shall we sit?" Abby asked. "Not near Mason, *please.*"

"Casey and I are eating lunch together," Hannah said. "We're going to work on our talent show act."

"Okay," Abby said. "I'll give advice."

"We, um, want to keep it a secret," Hannah said apologetically. She placed a carton of milk and a straw on her tray.

"I won't tell! I *promise*!"

Hannah looked uncomfortable. "We don't want anyone to know what we're doing — even you. Sorry! You don't mind, do you?"

"Of course not!" Abby said quickly. Her face turned red. "I'll go eat with Natalie and Bethany."

Hannah smiled at Abby. "I knew you'd understand!"

Abby paid the cashier. She picked up her tray and looked around the cafeteria. The tables were crowded with noisy groups of friends. No one was sitting alone.

Natalie and Bethany were together. Abby walked slowly toward them.

"You should approach center stage when I say 'Hark! Who goeth in the dark night?'" Natalie said to Bethany.

"How do I enter?" Bethany asked.

"You should skip lightly," Natalie said, "and scatter flowers around you."

"Hi," Abby said.

Natalie didn't even glance up.

"But when do I fall down in a faint?" Bethany protested.

"Hi," Abby said again.

"That's in the *next* act," Natalie said.

"You mean, when I'm holding Blondie? I don't want to hurt her!"

"She'll be in a cage. You'll put it down first," Natalie said.

Abby walked away. She sat down at the end of another table and began to eat her lunch.

At least she hadn't gotten the mashed potatoes.

How could she have eaten them, anyway, after listening to Zach and Mason talk about glue and grease?

"So, like, what are *you* doing for the talent show?" Victoria said, sitting down next to Abby.

"Are you talking to me?" Abby said.

"Is there anyone else here?" Victoria asked impatiently.

Victoria didn't often talk to Abby. Brianna was her only friend in Ms. Kantor's class. It was a good thing, Abby thought, that Brianna and Victoria *weren't* in the same class. No one would survive them together in one room all day long.

Abby took a long sip of chocolate milk before she answered Victoria's question. "Nothing," she finally said. "I'm not doing anything for the talent show."

Brianna sat down across from them. Her tray was heaped with food. She had mashed potatoes, meat loaf, french fries, and apple pie.

"It's because of me, isn't it, Abby?" Brianna said. "When there's a brilliant star onstage, the little people give up."

"Little people?" Victoria said. "Like, who do you mean?"

"Everyone!" Brianna said confidently, taking a big forkful of mashed potatoes. "I'm used to it, you know. People just fade away when I'm around. They become pathetic little satellites orbiting the sun."

"Oh, really?" Victoria said.

Abby glanced over at Hannah and Casey and sighed deeply. Then she pushed away her plate.

"I'm the best. Everyone knows it. Yay, Brianna!" Brianna cheered for herself. "I'm the blazing star that everyone envies."

"You'll be as round as the sun if you eat like a horse," Victoria warned.

"You're mixing your metaphors," Brianna corrected.

"What*ever*!"

"And I burn off calories faster than anyone I know," Brianna bragged. "I never gain weight." She dug her fork into the meat loaf.

Victoria slammed down her low-fat milk.

"I think I have a stomachache," Abby said to no one in particular.

Brianna turned to Abby again. "So? What's it like having Jessica back in town?"

"She's not here yet," Abby said in surprise. How did Brianna know that Jessica was about to visit?

"Yes, she is," Brianna said. "She flew in this morning."

Abby stared at her.

"Her flight plans got changed. I heard about it yesterday. My mother works with *her* mother's cousin's brother-in-law," Brianna said smugly. "Do you remember Jessica?" she asked Victoria.

"She, like, wears overalls and smiley-face buttons like she's in, like, some toddler television show," Victoria said.

"I don't think she dresses like that anymore," Abby said slowly.

"It's about time!" Victoria snapped.

"Are you sure Jessica's back?" Abby asked Brianna.

"I have the best information," Brianna said. "I'm *connected*."

Abby picked up her tray and stood up to leave. She felt a little breathless. Jessica was here *already*? Abby wasn't sure that she was ready to see her.

Chapter 4

Saturday night

"We are known by our
friends."

ID Card Calendar

<u>But do our friends know us?</u>

At two o'clock this afternoon, the doorbell rang.

I thought it was Hannah. She said
she might stop by after she and Casey
had rehearsed their act for the talent
show.

I ran downstairs, flung open the door,
and saw

<u>Jessy.</u>

Awkward Conversation #1

Me (can't say a word; staring with mouth open)

Jessy: Abby! I'm back! Hi!

Me: Um, uh, hi . . .

Mom (calling from the next room): Abby! Who is it?

Me: It's Jess-Jessic-Jessy!

Mom: Jessica?? Isn't she in Oregon?

Me: She's here, Mom.

Jessy: Hi, Mrs. Hayes.

Mom (arrives in hallway): Mrs. Hayes? Since when am I Mrs. Hayes?

Jessy: At my dad's, we address adults formally.

Mom: Here, I'm Olivia.

Jessy: Okay, Olivia.

Mom: Come on in! It's good to see you! We've missed you so much, haven't we, Abby!

Me: Uh, sure.

Jessy steps into the hallway. Now we can really see her.

The New, Improved Jessy

1. is wearing a teeny, tiny, tight top and a miniskirt with fat pink daisies,
2. <u>and</u> chunky, high-heeled shoes.
3. She has short, curly auburn hair,
4. shiny orange lips,
5. and <u>earrings!!!</u>

What Is Wrong with This Picture?

1. Jessica hates pink.
2. Jessica never wears skirts, especially miniskirts.
3. Jessica has long straight <u>brown</u> hair.
4. Jessica doesn't own tinted lip gloss.
5. Jessica promised we would get our ears pierced <u>together</u>!

AAAAAAAAAAAAAAAAAAAAAA AAAAAAAAAHHHHHHHH!!!!!!! Who <u>is</u> this person? I knew Jessica had changed into Jessy, but I never imagined it would be <u>this</u> bad! Has an alien taken her over? Has she transformed into another life-form?

Awkward Conversation #2

Mom: Don't you look nice! You've changed, haven't you?

Jessy: My mother thinks I've matured.

Abby: Uh.

Mom: When did you arrive?

Jessy: Yesterday. I wrote Abby that I was coming.

Mom: Why didn't you say anything about Jessica's visit, Abby?

Jessy: I'm Jessy now.

Abby: Well, uh . . .

Dad (arrives in hallway): Jessica?? Is that <u>you</u>?

Jessy: It's Jessy.

Dad: You've grown up, Jessy!

Jessy: Yes.

Mom: How long are you here? Can you and your mother come for dinner tonight? Why didn't you <u>tell</u> us, Abby? We'd have prepared something special. Oh, dear. Now it's so last minute. . . .

Abby: Um, uh, yeah.

Jessy: I don't <u>think</u> we have any plans for dinner.

She pulls a turquoise cell phone from her purse. (<u>Jessica carries a purse? And a cell phone?</u>)

Jessy: Mom? Any plans for tonight? The Hayeses have invited us for dinner. Okay? Okay.

She clicks off the phone and smiles at my parents.

Jessy: We're free.

Mom and Dad: Great!

Mom: That's settled. Now you and Abby can go play.

Abby: <u>Play?</u>

Awkward Conversation #3

(Note: This conversation takes place in Abby's room.)

Jessy (takes in purple walls, purple furniture, purple curtains and bedspread): Same old purple, huh?

Abby: Sure. It's my favorite color, like always.

Jessy: That's cool.

The two girls sit down. Abby sits on the floor; Jessy sits on the bed.

Abby: Do you still like science? And outer space? Do you still want to be an astronomer?

Jessy: No.

Abby: Oh. Too bad.

Jessy: Why?

Abby: I don't know. Do you still play soccer?

Jessy: Nah . . . it's messy.

Abby: Messy? What's Dakota like?

Jessy: My little stepsister? She's a brat.

Abby: I thought you wanted a younger sister.

Jessy (rolls her eyes): In my dreams. How's Natalie?

Abby: She and Bethany are good friends now.

Jessy: Oh.

Abby: What's Danielle like?

Jessy: She's so, so, so, like, you know, cool. . . .

Abby: Oh. Yeah.

Jessy: I knew you'd understand. Any cute guys in your class?

Abby: No.

Jessy (leans forward and lowers her voice): There's this boy named Ian.

Abby: So?

Jessy: He's kind of cute. He's in sixth grade.

Abby: Oh.

Jessy: He gave me a ring. We're going out together.

Abby: Whoa.

Jessy: Ian and I go to parties every weekend. Any parties here?

Abby: Not that I know of.

Jessy (sighs): Too bad.

Abby: What's that noise?

Jessy: My cell phone.

She pulls out the turquoise cell phone and flips it open.

T-Jeff walks into the room and jumps on my lap.

Abby (whispers): Hi, T-Jeff. You're still the same, aren't you?

T-Jeff (purrs loudly)

Jessy: Danielle! It's so cool that you called! I'm dying to talk to you! No, I'm not doing anything! I'm at Abby's. Uh-huh.

Sure, we're having a great time. Have you seen Ian? Does he miss me? Really? Are you <u>sure</u>?

Length of phone conversation: 17 minutes
Times Ian's name was mentioned: hundreds
Times Jessy asked if he missed her: 23
Other topics of conversation: shopping, clothes, parties, boys, dances, hair, makeup, clothes, boys, dances, parties
Times Jessy squealed or shrieked: 54
Times Jessy checked her nails while on phone: 16

Is this like the flu? Will she recover someday and be normal again?

I'm going to have to put out a special edition of the <u>Hayes Book of World Records</u> for this visit alone.

Jessy will get a Lifetime Achievement Award for Most Terribly Transformed Ten-Year-Old (Who Thinks She's a Teenager).

Chapter 5

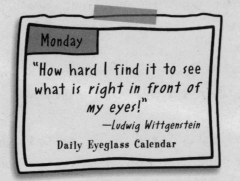

Monday

"How hard I find it to see
what is *right in front of*
my eyes!"
—Ludwig Wittgenstein

Daily Eyeglass Calendar

I could say the same about my family.

It is very hard for them to see what is right in front of their eyes.

I think they need eyeglasses, binoculars, or magnifying lenses.

How can they miss what's so plain to see?

<u>Can't they see how much Jessica has changed?</u>

Excuse me. How much <u>Jessy</u> has changed.

At dinner on Saturday night, everyone

acted like everything was exactly the way it used to be. Even her mom!!

The only thing they said was that Jessy had "grown up."

Is this what growing up means? Turning into a brainless, boy-crazy, gold-satin-tight-T-shirt-and-flowered-miniskirt-wearing, turquoise-cell-phone-carrying party lover?

<u>Then I don't want to grow up!!!!</u>

Everyone seemed really happy to see Jessy and her mom. (Her mom is one of the nicest moms ever.)

Everyone kept telling Jessy and me how happy and excited we must be to see each other again. Jessy always smiled and said yes. No one noticed that I didn't say much.

Jessy's mom said that she and Jessy were going to shop for new clothes, visit grandparents, and just spend time together this week. She said that we'd have plenty of time to see each other, as well.

"Of <u>course</u>," Jessy said.

"Yeah, sure," I mumbled.

Everyone thought it was lucky that our spring breaks fall at different times. That means Jessy can visit Ms. Kantor's class over the next few days.

That also means that Jessy will meet Hannah. And Hannah will meet Jessy.

Hannah will see and understand. Even if no one else does.

It was a hot spring day. Both fifth-grade classes were out on the high school track preparing to do the mile run. Mr. Stevens, the gym teacher, stood on the grass with a stopwatch in his hand.

"Five minutes of stretches!" he announced. "Then we'll run."

Abby pushed her curly hair out of her face, then leaned down and tightened the laces on her purple sneakers.

Natalie jogged over to her. "Jessica's back in town," she announced. "I saw her yesterday!"

"How was it?" Abby asked. "What was she wearing?"

"*What was she wearing?*" Bethany plopped down on the grass next to Abby and began doing sit-ups. "Have you *ever* seen Jessica in anything but overalls and a T-shirt?"

Abby leaned forward to touch her toes. "Well, yes, I have."

"Funny you should say that," Natalie said. "I thought she looked a bit different."

"A *bit different*?" Abby cried, jumping up. "She's turning into someone else!"

"Maybe she already *is* someone else," Bethany chirped.

Before Abby could say another word, Mr. Stevens blew his whistle. "Stretching time is over! Everyone at the starting line!"

Abby trotted around the track, trying to keep up a steady pace like Mr. Stevens had advised.

She didn't like running. And she wished she had had a chance to ask Natalie a few more questions.

Hadn't Natalie seen how changed Jessy was? Was Jessy wearing a big old coat over the miniskirt and tiny tank top? Or had she put on a wig, wiped off all the makeup, and worn her old clothes?

Or had Natalie been blindfolded when she saw Jessy?

Abby glanced at the other fifth-graders running around the track.

Brianna and Victoria were wearing matching zip-up velour sweatshirts and wide-legged sweatpants. Brianna's outfit was hot pink and Victoria's was lime green. They looked like two artificially colored candies.

Natalie and Bethany were sprinting past everyone else. Mason looked like he was running in place, but his face was already bright pink. It was almost the color of Brianna's velour suit.

"Mason, pick up the pace! Brianna! Victoria! Faster!" Mr. Stevens called. "This isn't Fifth Avenue! You're on a different kind of runway here!"

Abby smiled. Then her smile faded as she thought of Jessy. If Jessy were here, would she wear a turquoise velour sweat suit with floppy pant legs, just like Brianna and Victoria? Maybe Jessy would run with them instead of with Abby or Natalie.

Or maybe she'd talk to Danielle and Ian on her cell phone while she jogged.

Ahead of her on the track, Hannah and Casey were running together.

"Faster!" Mr. Stevens called, encouraging the slow ones. "You can do it!"

Abby put on a burst of speed. "Hannah! Casey! Wait!" she called. "Wait for me!"

Neither Hannah nor Casey responded.

"I hate jogging!" Abby muttered to herself. Her face was hot. "I feel like a tomato, and I probably look like one, too." She should have worn a cherry-colored velour sweat suit for the complete look: red hair, red face, and red clothing.

"That's the way, Abby!" Mr. Stevens said as she ran past him. "You're doing great!"

Now she couldn't slow down. She surged ahead. Hannah and Casey were closer.

"Hannah!" she called.

Hannah turned and waved. She had her usual huge smile. "Abby!" she cried in delight.

Abby felt better just looking at her. Hannah would understand everything.

"Hey, Hayes," Casey called.

"I've *got* to talk to you, Hannah!" Abby cried. "Slow down!"

Casey pretended to frown. "What about me?"

"Nope," Abby said. "Girls only."

"Awwwwww," Casey said. "Do I have to leave?"

"Not yet," Abby said, joining them. "You can stay in the sandbox," she added. It was a line from the story she had read to the class the other day.

Hannah and Casey started laughing.

"It's not *that* funny," Abby said.

"It was the way you said it," Hannah explained.

Abby fell into rhythm with her friends. "Okay." She shrugged. "Whatever." Then she pulled Hannah aside. "I've *got* to talk to you privately. And soon."

"Not now," Hannah said. She glanced at Casey.

"When?" Abby said. "It's urgent!"

"After school?" Hannah proposed.

"We're rehearsing," Casey reminded her.

"Oh, yeah, right," Hannah said to Casey. "And then you're having dinner at my house."

Abby felt a pang of regret. It could have been her having dinner with Hannah, if only she had wanted to be in the talent show.

"*Why* won't you tell me what your skit is about?" Abby said. "You know I can keep a secret."

Hannah and Casey looked at each other.

"We just can't," Hannah finally said.

"Sorry," Casey said. Then he added, "It's hilarious, Hayes. You're gonna love it."

"You will," Hannah agreed.

"Okay, I'm sure I will," Abby said. "But can we talk soon? It's really important."

"I'll call you tonight when we're done, Abby. I promise!"

Chapter 6

Wednesday

"Some things never change."
Four Seasons Calendar

Oh, yeah?

Things That Have Changed

1. Jessy: Duh!
2. Hannah's brain: She never, ever, ever, ever forgets to call me, but she did.
3. Hannah's schedule: She doesn't have a single free moment for me! She eats, sleeps, walks, and talks the talent show!
4. Casey and Hannah: They rehearse every minute of the day. They laugh all the time. I feel really left out!

5. Me: I've become invisible. Hannah
hardly notices me anymore. Maybe I
should do an act for the talent show,
after all — as the Incredible Invisible
Friend!

Is there anything that <u>hasn't</u> changed???!!!

When Jessy walked into Ms. Kantor's fifth-grade class after the late bell on Wednesday morning, there was a loud gasp.

"Wooo-eee!" Mason yelled.

"Who's tha —" Brianna began, and then closed her lips tightly.

"Jessica!" Bethany squealed. "You're back!"

Abby stared openmouthed at her former best friend. Somehow seeing her in school was even more shocking than seeing her at home.

Jessy was wearing a tiny orange miniskirt with a scoop-necked white lace top. She had rings on her fingers and a silver choker. Her lips gleamed suspiciously pink.

"Hubba, hubba," Zach said.

"Oh, shut up," Natalie said. "It's only Jessica."

"*Only?*" Zach repeated with a big grin on his face.

Hannah nudged Abby. "Is that really her? Jessy?"

Abby's face got hot. "She never used to look like *that*."

"She's cute," Hannah pronounced. "Jessy's better dressed than Brianna, don't you think?"

As if she had heard, Brianna pulled a lipstick out of her purse and began applying it furiously.

"What happened to the overalls?" Bethany suddenly wailed.

"Welcome back, Jessica!" Ms. Kantor greeted her with a smile and a hug. "We're really happy to have you with us today. We all want to hear about your new life in Oregon. But why don't you sit down now, so we can get started? It's time for social studies."

"I'm Jessy now," Jessy informed the class. She glanced in Abby's direction and gave a little wave. Then she began walking toward Abby.

"She's coming to sit *here*," Abby muttered.

Natalie frowned. "What's wrong with that? Didn't she always?"

Jessy greeted her former classmates like a visiting celebrity as she made her way through the classroom.

"Is there room for me here?" she asked Abby.

Abby nodded.

Hannah pointed to the seat between her and Abby. "Hi! I'm Hannah! I've been dying to meet you."

Jessy smiled at her. "Nice to meet you, too."

She reached into her purse, pulled out a pack of gum, and offered pieces to Abby and Hannah.

"Thanks!" Hannah said with a huge smile.

"Anytime." Jessy flipped open her cell phone.

"Don't let Ms. Kantor see that!" Abby warned.

"You brought a cell phone to school?" Brianna cried.

Jessy switched off the phone and slipped it into a pocket.

"Abby!" she whispered. "I got a phone call from Ian this morning! He said he went to a mad cool party! He said he missed me!"

" 'Mad cool'?" Abby repeated.

"You know, like crazy wicked, or mad good," Jessy explained.

"O-*kay*," Abby said.

She glanced over at Hannah to see if she had heard. But Hannah had taken out her social studies book and was flipping through the pages to find the assignment.

"What do you think of her?" Abby whispered to Hannah as they hurried down the hallway on their way to lunch.

"She's nice," Hannah said. "Really nice."

"Are you serious?"

Hannah looked surprised. "Of course I am."

"But her *clothes*!"

"I didn't think you cared that much about how people looked!"

"*You* didn't know her before. Now she talks about nothing but boys and parties! 'Mad cool' parties," Abby mimicked.

"She's not *that* bad," Hannah said, then broke off in midsentence. "Casey! Over here!" She turned to Abby. "I have to . . ."

". . . rehearse," Abby finished. "I know. See you later." She walked away before Hannah could make another promise she'd break.

Abby entered the lunchroom alone.

"Abby!" Bethany grabbed her arm. "Quick! Everyone wants to sit with Jessy. We saved a seat next to her for you!"

She pushed Abby into a seat between Jessy and Natalie. "Sit here," she ordered.

"All for one and one for all," Jessy said.

"Isn't that the Three Musketeers?" Abby asked. "There are four of us: you, me, Bethany, and Natalie."

46

"Actually five. I thought Hannah would be with you," Natalie explained. "We saved her a seat, too."

"She and Casey are rehearsing," Abby said.

"Too bad," Jessy said. "She seems really nice."

"She is," Abby answered. *When she's not rehearsing with Casey*, she added silently.

Victoria and Brianna appeared at the table, holding lunch trays.

"You, like, saved chairs for us, didn't you?" Victoria said.

"I'll sit *here*," Brianna said, pointing to the place that Natalie had saved for Hannah.

Victoria put her tray down on the table and sat down in the empty chair. "I'm first."

"No!" Brianna cried. "Jessy is *my* friend!"

Victoria clutched Jessy's arm. "But now she's, like, *mine*."

Jessy edged away. "I don't think so. . . ."

"We're saving that seat," Natalie interrupted.

"Like, for whom?" Victoria demanded.

Abby scanned the cafeteria. Hannah and Casey were sitting across the room at an almost empty table.

"Um," Natalie began. "Well, we were saving it for, for —"

"Ian," Jessy said loudly.

Victoria and Brianna exchanged glances. "We don't know any Ian."

"He's my boyfriend," Jessy said.

"You have a *boyfriend*?" Brianna gasped.

"Don't you?" Jessy answered.

Victoria stood up. "Like, aren't we supposed to, like, sit over there?" she said, pointing to another table.

"That's the best place," Brianna said.

The two girls picked up their trays and walked away.

"Wow! That got rid of them!" Natalie exclaimed.

"Pest control," Jessy said, with satisfaction. "You just need the right formula."

Jessy, Abby, and Natalie grinned at one another.

"Is Ian *really* here?" Bethany asked.

"I wish!" Jessy cried. She pulled out her cell phone and flipped it open. "I wonder if he's called me."

Abby sighed. For a fleeting moment, it had almost seemed like the old Jessica was back.

Chapter 7

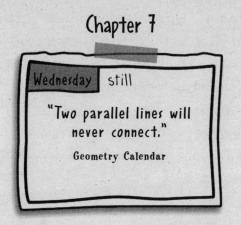

Wednesday still

"Two parallel lines will never connect."

Geometry Calendar

Jessy and I are like parallel lines. We are going in the same direction, but we don't connect.

I was starting to think that Hannah and I were like parallel lines, too. We never connect anymore!

But today after lunch, Hannah came up to me. "I'm sorry I haven't been around much," she said.

"That's okay," I mumbled.

"I know I've been spending all my time

with Casey," Hannah continued. "It's because of the skit! I can't wait for you to
see it — but you'll <u>have</u> to be patient." She
smiled. "It <u>has</u> to be a surprise."

I shrugged. "Sure, whatever."

"Maybe we can have a sleepover Saturday night?" Hannah said. "I haven't asked
my mother, but I know she'll say yes."

"Um, yeah," I said. "I think I can. I
mean, Jessy hasn't said anything about us
getting together."

"Great!" Hannah cried. She threw her
arms around me. "I was <u>hoping</u> you
weren't mad."

"Mad?" I said.

"You always seem upset when I go off
with Casey," Hannah explained.

"That's because I'm dying to talk to
you!" I burst out. "And you forgot to call
me back on Monday."

"Oh, no," Hannah said. "I'm sorry. But
wait until you see the skit!" she said for
the millionth time. "You're really going to
love it. <u>I'm</u> crazy about it."

"I <u>know</u>," I said.

We looked at each other and started to laugh.

"I thought you'd be glad that I was out of the way," Hannah said.

"<u>What?</u>"

"You know, since Jessy is here."

"I wish you were <u>around</u> when I'm with her!" I cried. "Jessy is so different. I don't know how to be with her anymore."

"Has she really changed <u>that</u> much?" Hannah asked.

"Yes," I said.

Hannah listened and didn't say much. But I felt as if she understood.

Hooray! Hooray! Hooray! Hannah and I have connected again. (We're not parallel lines anymore. Are we a circle?)

Now I don't have to worry that she's forgotten about me. I can't wait for Saturday!

"Do you want to come over?" Jessy asked Abby at the end of the day. "My mother baked brownies last night."

"Uh, yeah, I guess so," Abby said. She picked up her backpack and slung it over her shoulders. She had stayed after school for a few extra minutes to finish a math assignment, and now she and Jessy were the last ones left in the classroom.

Hannah had left with Casey to rehearse again. Natalie and Bethany had disappeared together, too. All her friends had gone, and only Jessy had waited for her.

Jessy looked pleased. "I wasn't sure you'd want to visit."

"I do," Abby protested. Then, wishing that she had been more enthusiastic, she added, "Your mother's brownies are the best!"

"They are," Jessy agreed. "I haven't had any that good in a long time."

The two girls waved good-bye to Ms. Kantor and walked down the hallway.

"So, how was it?" Abby said.

"How was what?"

"Being back for a day at good old Lancaster Elementary again."

"It was fine," Jessy said. "But my new school is so much bigger."

"Oh," Abby said.

They hurried out of the school and walked down the street.

"Everyone seems younger here," Jessy said.

"*You* seem older," Abby said.

Jessy pulled out her cell phone. "I'm used to a different crowd now."

"Are you going to check your messages *again*?" Abby cried. "How many times a day does Ian call you?"

Jessy cast an annoyed glance in Abby's direction. "You don't understand," she began. "What it's like to be in lo — "

"Why, *look*, Brianna!" Victoria said brightly, stepping in front of them on the sidewalk. "It's, like, *Jessy*!"

"*What* a surprise!" Brianna exclaimed. "We were just standing here talking about, uh . . ."

Victoria elbowed her. "Like, you know, we were discussing eye makeup, and whether, like, blue or, like, green eye shadow is more, like, you know . . ."

"You were waiting for me?" Jessy said in a cool tone.

"We wanted to see you alone," Brianna corrected. "Away from all those immature fifth-graders."

"I'm *not* alone now," Jessy reminded them, with a glance at Abby.

"Like, we couldn't talk to you with, like, Natalie there," Victoria said. "She's *soooo* pushy!"

Abby and Jessy glanced at each other.

"We want to, like, ask you about your clothes." Victoria eyed Jessy's miniskirt. "How much did you, like, pay for that skirt?"

Jessy rolled her eyes.

"And where did you get those shoes?" Brianna said. She knelt down to inspect them. "I've been looking for a pair just like them."

Victoria pinched the edge of Jessy's lace shirt. "Is this, like, cotton or a blend?"

Brianna stood up again. "You got your hair colored, didn't you?"

"I think you should, like, you know, come over to my house and we can, like, talk about this stuff," Victoria said.

"Abby and I have plans," Jessy said. "Sorry."

"Tell Abby to, like, go home!"

"No," Jessy said.

"Oh, well. Another time." Brianna flashed her movie-star smile at Jessy. "But before you go, tell us what the parties you go to are like."

"They're mad good," Abby said.

"Yeah," Jessy agreed. "I've told Abby all about them."

"Like *she* would understand," Victoria said sarcastically.

"You have to tell us about Ian. Is he cute? Is he popular? Is he a fifth-grader?" Brianna asked eagerly.

Reaching into her purse, Jessy pulled out a mini photo album and flipped it open. "Here," she said. "Look."

Victoria gasped. "That's *him*?"

"Let *me* see!" Brianna squealed, pushing Victoria out of the way.

Abby craned her neck. All she could see was a blur of a boy's face.

"Well!" Brianna stepped back. She smoothed her hair and put her hands on her hips. "You've done nicely for yourself, haven't you, Jessy?"

Victoria scowled. "He doesn't, like, know what a nerd *Jessica* used to be," she snapped, "with those, like, farmer overalls and smiley-face buttons."

"Shut up!" Abby cried.

Victoria smiled meanly.

"Let's go, Victoria." Brianna turned to Jessy one last time. "If you want to hang with us, this is your final chance!"

Jessy shook her head.

Brianna and Victoria linked arms and swayed down the street, singing "Nasty Sugar Sweet," their favorite Tiffany Crystal tune.

Abby sighed with relief. "Thank goodness they're gone!"

"I think that Victoria has a grin like a crocodile," Jessy said.

"Or an alligator," Abby corrected.

"Something with sharp teeth that crawls on its stomach, lives in a swamp, and eats poor helpless little animals," Jessy said.

"That describes Victoria exactly," Abby agreed.

"I feel sorry for her parents," Jessy said.

"And her sisters and brothers," Abby continued, "and her neighbors and her classmates."

"I wonder what would happen if Victoria had to be nice for one whole day," Jessica said.

"She'd explode," Abby said. "She was born to be mean."

"Maybe we should get her a T-shirt saying that," Jessy joked. " 'Born to Be Mean.' "

"Only if it's a designer T-shirt," Abby said. "And we'll have to get a matching T-shirt for Brianna that says 'Born to Be *Me*.' "

The two girls had reached the entrance to the park.

"Remember how we used to Rollerblade here all the time?" Abby said.

"That was fun," Jessy said. "Too bad I don't have my Rollerblades with me." She paused for a moment. "Maybe we can go swimming together this weekend."

"Sure," Abby said. "I'd love to."

"I'll ask my mother when — " Jessy stopped abruptly. "Oooooh, *love*birds!"

Abby didn't turn around. "Is that *all* you think about?"

"So?" Jessy said. "They remind me of Ian and me." She pulled out her cell phone.

"Not again!" Abby groaned. "Please!"

Jessy gazed hopefully at the display on her phone, then sighed and put it away. "No messages. Look, they're holding hands! Isn't it romantic?"

"I don't even want to see it," Abby said.

"They're in love," Jessy continued. "I can tell."

"Ugh," Abby said. "Love." In spite of herself, she glanced in the direction of the couple. They were sitting some distance away on a park bench.

"Let's go that way," Jessy said, pointing to a path that led to a small lake.

Abby couldn't answer her. Her mouth had gone dry. Her heart was pounding wildly.

Yes, it was them. There was no mistaking the boy and girl holding hands, even at this distance. It was Casey and Hannah.

Chapter 8

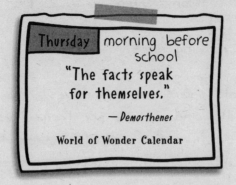

Facts

1. Casey and Hannah were sitting on a park bench,

2. gazing into each other's eyes,

3. holding hands,

4. and not aware of anything or anyone around them.

More Facts

1. I turned and ran out of the park.

2. I didn't say another word to Jessy.

3. I ran until I reached my house.

4. I pretended I was sick and couldn't come to the phone when Jessy called.

There's nothing more to say.

The facts speak for themselves. The facts speak loudly and clearly for themselves. In fact, the facts are shouting! (I wish the facts would shut up, already.)

Questions
1. What does this mean?
2. Will Hannah start carrying a cell phone and checking it every two seconds for messages from Casey?
3. Will she start wearing miniskirts?
4. Will she forget about all the things she once liked?

At least I know she won't get her ears pierced! Her mother won't let her. Just like mine. (Ha-ha-ha-ha-ha! For once, I am grateful for strict mothers!)

I don't want Hannah to change, too!!!

Even though Jessy is still a nice person, she's not the same!

More Questions

1. Will I have to explain to Jessy why I ran away from the park?
2. Will she understand how I feel about Hannah and Casey?
3. Is she angry that I didn't go over to her house yesterday?
4. Is she mad that I refused to come to the phone when she called afterward?

Even More Questions

1. Will Casey stop playing basketball with me?
2. Will he and Hannah walk to school by themselves for the rest of the year?
3. Will I lose all of my friends in one day???

(That would break every record in the Hayes Book of World Records!!!)

Yes, Even More Questions

1. Can I cancel the sleepover with Hannah on Saturday night? (<u>I don't want to go!!!</u>)

2. If I go, will Hannah talk nonstop about Casey?

3. Or will she say <u>nothing</u> about Casey?

4. Which would be worse: Talking about him or <u>not</u> talking about him??

Help! Help! Help!

HELP!

Chapter 9

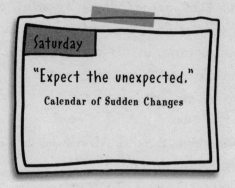

Saturday

"Expect the unexpected."

Calendar of Sudden Changes

If I expect the unexpected, then it's expected; and the unexpected must be the expected, right? Oh, NEVER MIND!

The unexpected keeps right on happening, whether it's expected or not.

Sudden Sleepover Switcheroo

Hannah canceled our Saturday night sleepover.

Jessy invited me for a Saturday night sleepover.

•　＊　•

Hannah's little sister, Elena, has a stomach virus. Her mother doesn't want anyone sleeping over while Elena is sick. Hannah slipped me a note in school yesterday that said, "Maybe next weekend instead?"

I wrote back, "Maybe."

I am relieved that I don't have to spend time with Hannah!

I am grateful that I didn't have to cancel the sleepover.

Hannah was very friendly in school yesterday. She acted like nothing had happened. If I hadn't seen her and Casey on the park bench together, I never would have guessed.

But at lunchtime, when she and Casey sat together, I saw them in a whole new light. I used to think they were obsessed with their act for the talent show; now it looks like they are obsessed with each other.

I am nervous about spending time with Jessy.

She doesn't seem upset that I ran away in the park and wouldn't even talk to her on the phone afterward. The old Jessica would have been angry. Why isn't Jessy?

What are Jessy and I going to do together for a whole afternoon and evening? What will we talk about?

Even though I'm not looking forward to the sleepover with Jessy, I'm relieved that I have plans for the weekend. I don't have to be alone, wondering about Casey and Hannah.

Jessy slammed her locker door and picked up her swim cap and goggles from the bench. "Are you ready?" she asked Abby.

"Not quite," Abby said, unbuttoning the top button of her shirt. "Why don't you go ahead?"

"Okay," Jessy said. "I'll see you in the pool." She sauntered toward the showers in a tiny blue bikini that Brianna and Victoria would have envied.

It was the evening of the sleepover. The two girls had come to the town pool to swim. In an hour or so, Jessy's mother was going to pick them up and take them out for pizza.

Abby hung up her shirt and slipped her feet into flip-flops. Her own purple swimsuit was faded and stretched out. She picked up her towel and followed Jessy.

Jessy did a surface dive to the bottom of the pool. Her feet waved above the surface of the water. In a moment, she emerged triumphantly.

"I did a handstand!" she cried.

"Fantastic!" Abby said.

"It's the first time I've ever . . ." Jessy suddenly stopped. "Cute guys," she whispered. "Straight ahead!"

"I am *so* not interested," Abby groaned.

"You will be," Jessy said smugly.

Abby submerged herself underwater. Her red hair floated wildly around her face. She swam along the bottom of the pool for several moments.

It was only the beginning of their sleepover. Was she going to have to listen to this the entire time?

"Do you think we'll see Brianna and Victoria again?" Jessy asked when Abby came up for air.

"I hope not." Abby glanced around the pool, as if Brianna and Victoria might suddenly pop out from behind a stack of kickboards.

Jessy floated on a yellow Styrofoam noodle. "I wonder if Ian called," she said.

"If they made waterproof cell phones, you'd be able to check," Abby said.

"As soon as they invent one, I'm buying it," Jessy promised.

Abby turned on her back and floated with her arms outstretched. She almost wished for Brianna and Victoria to show up. Then the old Jessica might return — for a little while, at least.

"Have you ever been in the sauna?" Jessy asked suddenly.

Abby shook her head.

"Let's go check it out."

"I want to do some laps," Abby said. "Besides, isn't it hot in there?"

"Come on, Abby," Jessy pleaded. "It's *soooo* relaxing. Danielle and I went with Elizabeth. That's my stepmom," she explained. "But we can't stay in longer than ten or fifteen minutes. Otherwise we'll get fried."

"Crispy critters. Sounds like fun," Abby grumbled. But she followed Jessy out of the pool.

* * *

"Are you *sure* this is okay?" Abby asked as she and Jessy stepped into the sauna. "The sign on the door says it's only for women and girls over twelve."

Jessy waved her objections away. "No one else is here. And anyway, we're almost eleven, aren't we?"

"You can pass for twelve, but I can't," Abby protested.

"Don't worry." Jessy sat down on her towel and began to rub lemon-scented lotion onto her arms and legs. "If anyone asks, let me do the talking."

Abby leaned back against the wall and let the heat of the sauna wash over her. It was like being on a beach on a hot August day — except that the room was small and dark. "Isn't this great?" Jessy said.

"It's not bad," Abby admitted.

Jessy stretched out on her towel and closed her eyes.

For a while, neither girl said anything.

"Do you ever get lonely or scared?" Jessy asked suddenly.

"Of course." Abby thought of seeing Hannah and Casey on the park bench. She had felt both lonely *and* scared.

"That's how I felt when I got to my father's house."

Abby sat up and listened quietly. She had never heard Jessy talk about her feelings like this before — even when they were best friends and Jessy was Jessica.

Jessy adjusted her position on the towel. "But soon, Danielle and I became really close," she continued, "so I loved being there."

"That's good," Abby said.

"But *then* Danielle got a boyfriend," Jessy said, "and she forgot all about me."

"Oh, no."

"I felt so left out. All of a sudden, I was on my own in a new school."

"That must have been hard."

"It was," Jessy admitted. She took a breath. "So I made a few friends and got involved in some activities. And Danielle and her boyfriend broke up. Then Ian and I got together."

"Is she jealous of you and Ian?"

"She has another boyfriend now."

"Whoa," Abby said. It was hard to imagine one boyfriend, much less two. And it was even harder to imagine all the changes that Jessy had gone through. "No wonder you changed your name."

Jessy shrugged and didn't say anything.

"How are things now with Danielle?" Abby asked.

"Now that we both have boyfriends, it's much better." Jessy sat up on the bench.

"*I'm* not getting a boyfriend," Abby said, more to herself than to Jessy.

"You'll see," Jessy said, with a sly smile.

"No," Abby said.

"What about Casey and Hannah?" Jessy asked suddenly. "They spend a lot of time together."

"So?" Abby said. "They're rehearsing."

"*Rehearsing*," Jessy repeated, with a smile.

"You don't understand."

"*You're* the one who doesn't understand," Jessy said.

"They're both my friends," Abby insisted. "That's *all*. I want them to stay that way."

Jessy thought for a moment. "Hannah seems really nice. But she should fix up her look."

"Hannah doesn't care about her look!" Abby cried. She hoped it was still true; she hoped that Hannah hadn't turned into a Brianna clone overnight.

It seemed as if almost anything could happen these days.

The door opened and two middle-aged women came in. They frowned at Abby and Hannah.

"You girls shouldn't be in here," one of the women warned.

Jessy and Abby scrambled to their feet.

"We're just, just . . ." Abby stammered.

"We're leaving now," Jessy finished.

"It's against the rules," the other woman said. "I ought to report you to the desk."

Abby grabbed her towel and ran out the door. Jessy was right behind her.

"We weren't even in there for ten minutes," Jessy grumbled.

"We were about to turn into lobsters, anyway," Abby pointed out as she caught sight of her rosy face in the mirror.

"So what?" Jessy said. "I wasn't ready to go. If Elizabeth had been here, she would have let us stay!"

"Lobsters don't look good in miniskirts," Abby joked. She glanced quickly at Jessy. Would she be annoyed or bored by Abby's humor?

To her surprise, Jessy laughed. "I've missed you, Abby!" she cried.

Chapter 10

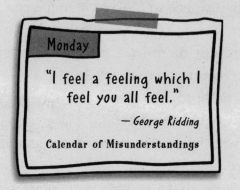

Monday

"I feel a feeling which I feel you all feel."

— *George Ridding*

Calendar of Misunderstandings

I feel so many feelings. If you feel what I feel, you're probably feeling that you have too many feelings.

WARNING! DO NOT READ ANY MORE OF THIS JOURNAL ENTRY IF YOU CAN'T STAND CONFUSION AND CONTRADICTION.

Miscellaneous Feelings Experienced in Jessy's Company: happiness, caring, friend-ship, boredom, irritation, anger, delight, fun, impatience, misunderstanding, sadness, fear, relief, laughter, loneliness

How can Jessy be so irritating and at the same time so nice?

How is it that we have nothing in common, but we still really like each other?

How can I really care about her and be so bored by her sometimes?

How can we have fun together and not really understand each other?

How can we have so many misunderstandings and still have a friendship?

We sort of had a good time at her house, even though she showed me pictures of Ian at least six or seven times. (It seemed like sixty or seventy.)

What's the big deal about Ian? He's not any better looking than Casey. Not that I think Casey is good-looking. I <u>don't</u>.

Jessy showed me pictures of Danielle, too, in her skating outfit. Danielle looks like a dancer. She is very tiny and has long legs and arms. She looks graceful. Brianna would be so jealous if she saw Danielle!

It was fun seeing Jessy's mother. Her mother is moving this summer to be near Jessy! She's found a new job and an apartment. Jessy won't be coming back here anymore. This might be the last time I ever see her.

Jessy is leaving in three days. I feel sad and relieved at the same time.

On Tuesday morning, the doorbell rang as Abby was getting ready to go to school.

"Come in!" she yelled.

The door opened. "Hey, Hayes," Casey said.

"Is that you? *Casey?*" Abby said in shock.

"Last time I checked," Casey joked. He pretended to pinch himself. "Yep. It's still me."

"Ha-ha. Very funny. Where's Hannah?"

Casey made a gagging motion. "Stomach flu."

"Ugh," Abby said. "Is she really sick?"

"Her mother said she threw up all night," Casey said.

"I'm glad I didn't sleep over this weekend. Otherwise I might be sick, too." Abby leaned down to double knot her sneakers.

"I spent a *lot* of time with her Saturday and Sunday." Casey shrugged. "But so what? I never get sick."

"You spent all weekend hanging out with Hannah?" Abby said. "She canceled on *me*."

"We were rehearsing, Hayes. At my house."

"Oh," Abby said. Somehow that didn't make her feel any better. Why hadn't Hannah asked if she could go to *Abby's* house on Saturday night instead? Was Hannah's sister's illness an excuse to spend more time with Casey?

They walked out the front door and headed toward school.

"So, um, how's the talent show skit?" Abby asked. "It must be incredible. All you and Hannah do is rehearse." (*And hold hands on park benches,* she added silently.)

"It's wonderful!" Casey said.

"Really?"

"Terrific, fantastic, and out of this world!"

"Can't you tell me *anything* about it?" Abby begged. "Just a hint? I'm dying of curiosity!"

"The performance is less than a week away," Casey replied. "And you *know* it's a secret. I'll say one thing: You'll be stunned, shocked, and completely surprised. You'll see."

Abby stared at him in dismay. What were he and Hannah planning to do? Make a public declaration of love?

At least she was the only one in Ms. Kantor's class who had seen them holding hands. So far.

"Great," she finally mumbled. "I'm happy for you. And Hannah, too."

Casey didn't reply. He just smiled mysteriously.

"Look at the lovebirds," Victoria said as Abby and Casey walked onto the playground. "Aren't they, like, *sweet*?"

"Tweet, tweet," Abby said.

"Ignore her," Casey said under his breath.

They headed toward the school entrance. Victoria followed them.

Brianna was talking to Bethany. Or rather, she was talking *at* Bethany.

"I got five standing ovations," Brianna bragged. "And sixteen bouquets of flowers. And twenty-seven cards."

Bethany yawned. "My hamster wiggled his whiskers two hundred and fifteen times in a row last night."

"That *doesn't* compare to my performance," Brianna insisted.

Victoria joined in the conversation.

"Have you seen Abby and Casey, Lancaster Elementary's newest couple?" she asked Brianna in a loud voice. "Hannah must be, like, so totally jealous!"

Bethany and Abby exchanged glances.

"Come *on*," Bethany said. "Abby's not Casey's girlfriend and Hannah's not—"

"It's, like, two girlfriends in, like, one week," Victoria interrupted. "That must be some kind of, like, record."

"Why don't you make like a tree and leave?" Casey said to her.

"Really?" Brianna asked eagerly. "Casey has *two*

girlfriends who are friends with each other?"

Casey rolled his eyes.

"We're all just *friends*," Abby protested.

"It's, like, so totally romantic," Victoria cried triumphantly. "I saw Casey and Hannah, like, holding hands the other day. They're crazy about each other. Like, who would think that *Casey* . . ." She suddenly stopped. "Now Abby's jealous, too."

"I am not jealous!"

"Let's go up to the library." Casey grabbed Abby's arm and pulled her into the school.

Victoria's taunting voice followed them. *"Jealous!"*

"Don't pay any attention to her," Casey said soothingly. "You know Victoria. She'll say anything."

"But what about, you know, you and Hannah?" Abby stammered. "Like, holding hands and all that stuff. Is it true?"

Casey looked disgusted. "Victoria *loves* to torment people."

When Abby didn't reply, he said, "Hannah and I are *not* going out together. We *don't* hold hands like boyfriend and girlfriend. I promise."

Abby tried to smile. But she felt sick inside.

It was one thing to lie to Victoria and Brianna. Sometimes you had to, for self-protection. It was another thing to lie to your closest friends.

Why wasn't Casey telling her the truth?

Chapter 11

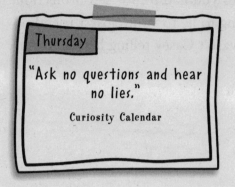

Thursday

"Ask no questions and hear no lies."

Curiosity Calendar

Why didn't I read this <u>before</u> I talked to Casey?

If I hadn't asked about him and Hannah, he wouldn't have lied.

My feelings wouldn't have been hurt.

I wouldn't have wondered what he was hiding.

I would have <u>still</u> been upset about him and Hannah.

But at least I wouldn't have felt that I could never trust him again!

(Question: What kind of a name is Vegetius? It sounds like an eggplant or a turnip.)

And why didn't I read this quote before I became friends with:

1. Jessy?
2. Hannah?
3. Casey?

I can't trust my friends at all.

Are they still my friends if they become boyfriend and girlfriend behind my back?

Are they still my friends if they suddenly lose interest in everything we used to have in common?

Are they still my friends if they lie to me?

"Make new friends, but keep the old. One is silver and the other gold."

Precious Metals Calendar

I refuse to say <u>anything</u> about this quote.

I'll write my own quote today:

"Watch out for your friends, old or new. They might disappoint, hurt, or lie to you."

— Abby Hayes

Completely Cranky Calendar

WAAAAAAAAAA! I don't _want_ to distrust my friends. I need my friends. I love my friends!

Yes, it's true. I admit it. I love my friends. Why do they do all these things?

Chapter 12

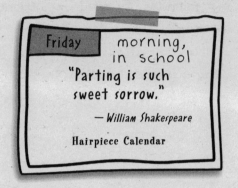

Friday morning,
in school
"Parting is such
sweet sorrow."

— *William Shakespeare*

Hairpiece Calendar

Parting is such <u>bitter</u>sweet sorrow. Jessy is gone. Will I ever see her again? Do I <u>want</u> to ever see her again?

We said good-bye at my house yesterday morning. Jessy gave me her cell phone number and said to call her.

She said it was "mad good" to see me. Her mother took a picture of the two of us with her digital camera. We stood in front of my house. Afterward, she showed us the picture. I looked eight years old. Jessy looked fourteen.

Jessy said she'd show the picture to Danielle, Ian, and all her new friends. (Yeah, right.)

But when it was time to go to the airport and they got in their car and drove away, I started crying. Just a little bit.

Mom said, "Don't worry, you'll see each other again."

Dad said, "Maybe you can visit Jessy in the summer."

(Maybe I <u>can</u>, but do I <u>want</u> to?)

Isabel said, "Maybe you'll be pen pals."

"Pen pals?" I said. "Aren't they usually strangers?"

"Why not have one who's a friend?" Isabel said.

"Why not?" I said slowly.

Jessy's changed so much, she's practically a stranger, anyway.

I'm in school right now, writing while everyone else reads.

Hannah is back. She looks and acts the same — no miniskirts, tight T-shirts, colored lip gloss, or cell phones yet. Thank goodness!

I'm glad she and Casey are still rehearsing all the time. I don't want to ask anything that would make Hannah lie to me.

I don't think I could stand that.

Ms. Kantor just announced that silent reading period is over. (I did silent writing. It's _practically_ the same.)

She said we have to talk about the talent show tomorrow night.

I don't want to _talk_ about the talent show. I don't want to _hear_ about the talent show. I don't want to _see_ the talent show. I don't want to get anywhere _near_ the talent show.

I think I'll have a mysterious wasting illness tomorrow night.

Or be abducted by aliens.

Or get sucked into a time warp and end up in the future a week from now.

Ms. Kantor is asking for volunteers for setup, cleanup, and ticket selling.

I refuse to be a volunteer. I will not be a volunteer. I <u>won't</u> be a vol –

Ms. Kantor asked all of us who aren't in the show to help out. She said she especially needed a responsible and trustworthy person for ticket selling.

Then she looked straight at me and said, "What about you, Abby?"

"Me?" I said, looking around for an escape.

"You're very responsible and trustworthy. Will you sell tickets the night of the talent show?"

How could I say no?

I'm selling tickets.

"Two tickets, please," said Abby's father. He held out a five-dollar bill.

"That'll be four dollars," Abby said, handing her father a couple of tickets and a one-dollar bill.

"Keep the change," Paul Hayes said, giving her back the dollar.

Abby grinned. "Thanks, Dad!"

"We'll save you a seat," her mother promised.

"Okay," Abby said, without enthusiasm. She wasn't looking forward to the talent show. Did she really have to watch Casey and Hannah onstage together?

They had come in earlier, whispering and laughing. Casey was in his normal clothes and Hannah was, too. They were both wearing jeans and T-shirts and sneakers. Were they planning to change into their costumes later?

Abby really didn't want to see this.

And what was going to happen *after* the show? Would things go back to the way they once were? Or would Casey and Hannah find more excuses to spend all their time together?

"Selling tickets?" said a loud, friendly voice. "I thought you'd be onstage. Or writing plays."

Abby smiled at Mason's mother, Betsy. "Not this time."

"Can't wait to see the show," Betsy said, handing her two dollars. "Mason is reciting a poem."

"That's amazing," Abby said.

Betsy laughed. "It is."

"What kind of a poem is it?" Abby asked.

"He wouldn't tell me." Betsy shrugged. "Mothers are the last to know."

And friends, too, Abby added silently.

"Where are my posters?" Brianna demanded, coming up to Abby.

She was dressed entirely in gold and silver: hair ribbons, necklace, earrings, stockings, slippers, ballet outfit, even her face powder and eye shadow.

"How should I know?" Abby waved to Betsy, who headed toward the gym. "I'm in charge of tickets, not posters."

Brianna gave a long, exasperated sigh.

"Brianna! Ouch! You're too bright!" Mason yelled, pretending to shield his eyes. "Where are my sunglasses?"

"Hush, Mason," Ms. Kantor said.

"Ms. Kantor!" Brianna cried. "My posters! They're not up!"

Their teacher sighed. "What posters, Brianna?"

Brianna reached into a large gold bag and took out a black-and-white poster. *"These,"* she said, pointing dramatically with a long, gold-polished fingernail.

Abby leaned forward to look. The poster was a larger-than-life photograph of Brianna's face with the words BRIANNA: THE SHOW written in block letters above. BRIANNA, SIMPLY THE BEST! was written below.

"*Someone* was supposed to put them up," Brianna said accusingly.

"I never promised that, Brianna!" Ms. Kantor said. "This isn't City Theater. No one has posters up. We can't make an exception for you."

"But I'm exceptional!" Brianna cried.

Mason cleared his throat. He seemed about to make a rude remark, but Victoria interrupted him.

"You're, like, all in *gold*!" she hissed at Brianna.

"So?" Brianna said.

"You promised me you were wearing *white*!" Victoria herself was wearing black. "If I had known you were, like, going, like, totally gold, I'd have, like . . ." Her voice sputtered furiously.

"*Yes?*" Brianna said. "Your point is?"

"Black and gold?" Victoria hissed. "We won't, like, look right together. This is so, like, totally wrong."

"Deal with it," Brianna said coldly. "The show must go on."

Victoria's eyes narrowed. "You . . ." she began.

Brianna turned her back on her friend and addressed Ms. Kantor. "If I can't put up these posters now," she announced, "I'll sell autographed copies after the performance."

"No, Brianna," Ms. Kantor said.

"But my fans will be so disappointed!" Brianna cried.

Victoria smiled nastily. "Deal with it."

"I won't take no for an answer," Brianna insisted. "And neither will my fans."

Ms. Kantor checked her watch. "We have ten more minutes until the show starts. Everyone, get backstage. Except you, Abby," she added. "You count the money and bring it to me."

Brianna continued to argue with Ms. Kantor as they headed toward the gym. Her voice carried all the way down the hall.

Abby opened the cash box. It was overflowing with dollar bills. She counted them, put them in an envelope, sealed it, and wrote the amount on the outside. Then she went to find her teacher.

"All counted, Ms. Kantor," Abby said, handing her the envelope.

"Good job." Ms. Kantor put the money in her jacket pocket. "Now, hurry up and take your seat. The show is about to begin."

Chapter 13

My fellow fifth-graders did not hide their talents. Or their lack of talents.

<u>Dumb Dances Done to Loud Music</u>: Too many.

<u>Most Bloodthirsty Act</u>: Mason, of course. He recited a long, gory poem about a battle. He read it very dramatically, especially the bloody parts.

"Isn't it amazing that he memorized that long poem?" someone behind me said.

No, it's <u>disgusting</u>! Why do people write

poems about war and death, anyway?

And why didn't Ms. Kantor stop him? She didn't look happy when he got to the part about hacked-off heads.

Most Interesting Interpretation: Natalie and Bethany's fantasy novel scene.

Bethany was a princess who spent half her time doing headstands and somersaults and the other half petting her hamster. Natalie was a prince. She wore a cape and painted sneakers, performed chemistry experiments, and used her sword to mix concoctions. (Okay, it was strange. But good, anyway.)

Most Original, Funny, AND Boring Idea: Zach and Tyler set up computer keyboards at opposite ends of the stage. Then they turned on a tape recorder. They had recorded the sound of a computer keyboard and amplified it. Zach and Tyler pretended to "play" their computers. It was funny at first. After ten minutes, it wasn't funny at all.

All That Glitters Isn't Gold Award: Brianna glittered in gold <u>and</u> silver. She sang, danced, and recited. At the end of her act, Victoria came to join her onstage.

<u>Worst Performing Pair</u>: Victoria and Brianna. Victoria looked like a big clumsy bug next to Brianna. To make things worse, Brianna kept getting in front of Victoria and upstaging her.

<u>Most Astonishing Moment</u>: Victoria scowled more and more angrily. She kept trying to regain center stage. Finally, she shoved Brianna. Hard.

Brianna didn't miss a beat. She danced nimbly out of the way, as if she had choreographed it. Victoria lost her balance and fell on her face.

<u>Undeniably Unforgettable Aftermath</u>: Victoria got up and stomped off the stage, yelling, "You'll be, like, <u>so totally</u> sorry!"

Brianna finished her dance and bowed deeply, to enthusiastic applause.

Victoria ran back onstage. "You stole the show from me!" she accused.

Brianna kept smiling and bowing.

The audience kept applauding.

(Did they think that Brianna and Victoria did this on purpose? I know they didn't! So does the rest of the fifth grade.)

Finally, Ms. Kantor ordered them off. The curtain came down. After a few minutes, it rose again, to reveal . . .

Casey and Hannah.

Hannah's hair was in pigtails. She had rolled up the cuffs of her jeans, and she was wearing yellow polka-dot socks. Casey was wearing a baseball cap.

<u>Most Hideous, Heartbreaking, Horrible Moment:</u> They stood in the middle of the stage holding hands. They were both smiling.

<u>Most Totally Embarrassed Audience Member</u>: Me.

<u>How Many Ways Was I Embarrassed?</u>
<u>Let Me Count the Ways</u>

1. Seeing two of my best friends holding hands in public, onstage, in front of our entire class, the rest of Lancaster Elementary School, our neighbors, our city, state, country, and the whole UNIVERSE.

2. Hearing my mother murmur, "Aren't they sweet?"

3. Watching Brianna and Victoria gape in astonishment.

4. Do I really need another one?

Casey and Hannah dropped each other's hands (THANK GOODNESS!) and stepped forward and began to speak.

<u>Most Astonishing, Awesome,</u>
<u>Amazing Announcement</u>
Casey and Hannah: Our skit today is

based on a story written by our friend and classmate Abby Hayes.

Together Casey and Hannah held up the sheet of paper. It said, "IN THE SANDBOX" BY ABBY HAYES, WITH A LITTLE HELP FROM CASEY AND HANNAH.

Size of My Surprise: Gigantic, tremendous, huge, vast, enormous, boundless, infinite.

Then Casey and Hannah acted out a skit about two five-year-olds playing in a sandbox. They fought over plastic shovels, made up, held hands (!), raced around the sandbox, built a sand castle together, and then wrecked it. It was a lot like the story I had read for my oral report.

The audience loved it.

I laughed so hard, I almost cried.

More Reasons I Might Have Cried

1. From relief.

2. From embarrassment. How could I have misunderstood so badly?

3. From happiness. My friends did this for <u>me</u>?

At the end, Hannah and Casey got a standing ovation. They gestured to me to join them onstage. I didn't have any hesitation. I ran up. The three of us grabbed each other's hands and bowed to the audience.

Chapter 14

Saturday (still)

"......"

Nothingness Calendar

I got lots of compliments after the talent show on my "collaboration" with Casey and Hannah.

"It was nothing," I kept on saying. "It was really nothing."

Ms. Kantor said, "But you wrote the script."

"Yeah," I agreed. "Sort of. I think."

"Without your story, there wouldn't have been a script," Ms. Kantor said. "You provided the inspiration and many of the ideas."

I turned to Hannah and said, "But why

didn't you just <u>ask</u> me for the story?"

"It was more fun to surprise you," she said.

"Were you surprised?" Casey asked.

"YES," I cried. "It was great! Once I understood what you were doing."

Hannah and Casey grinned at each other. "What did you think we were doing?" Hannah asked me.

"Uh, well," I stammered. "I, um, didn't know."

(There is NO WAY I am ever going to tell Casey and Hannah that I thought they were boyfriend and girlfriend.)

"We fooled her," Casey said with satisfaction.

"You were our invisible skit partner, Abby," Hannah added. "I bet you didn't know that."

"I felt pretty invisible," I agreed.

"I'm sorry!" Hannah hugged me. "But now you know why, don't you?"

I nodded.

If they had just asked me for the story, none of the misunderstandings would have happened. But then I wouldn't have had such a terrific surprise, either.

"I feel an ice-cream sundae craving coming on," Casey said. "I'm having an urge for chocolate peanut butter ice cream with whipped cream and cookies on top."

"That's funny," Hannah said. "That's exactly what my mother bought this afternoon." She gave Casey a friendly shove. "How did you know?"

"I'm a mind reader."

"Yeah, <u>right</u>!" Hannah and I said at the same time. Then we both started giggling.

"We're having an ice-cream sundae celebration at my house in half an hour," Hannah said to me. "You better be there, Abby!"

"<u>I'll be there!!!</u>" I said.

I let out a sigh of relief. My friends were back. And we were all together.

THE END

The AMAZING DAYS of ABBY HAYES

Abby's graduating from fifth grade. Is she ready for middle school?

Finding the perfect graduation outfit is the first thing Abby's worried about as she prepares to leave the fifth grade. She also has to survive a summer with an unexpected guest. And she has sixth grade on her mind — new classmates, tougher classes, and a different school! Can Abby handle so many changes all at once?

0-439-48282-8	Abby Hayes Super Special #1: The Best is Yet to Come	$5.99
0-439-63775-9	Abby Hayes Super Special #2: Knowledge is Power	$5.99

Coming Soon to Bookstores Everywhere!

AHSST

MAGIC ISN'T EASY...

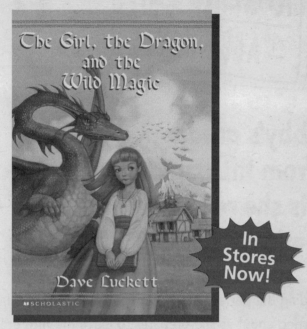

by Dave Luckett
Book One of the Rhianna Chronicles

Rhianna is failing out of magic school. She's very clumsy, even though she tries really hard. After she causes her biggest mess ever, a wizard appears with some astonishing news — Rhianna's magic is, in fact, stronger than anyone else's. She's a Wild Talent, which means that she possesses a pure form of magic that is full of power and energy.

The hitch? Well, it's very hard to control the wild magic. And it tends to suck up all the other magic around it. So when a dragon comes to town, it's up to Rhianna to save the day... if she can.

RC1T

Ella. Snow. Rapunzel. Rose.
Four friends who wait for no prince.

from best-selling authors
Jane B. Mason and Sarah Hines Stephens

With her feet bare (those glass slippers don't fit), and her second-hand gown splattered with mud (thanks, evil stepsisters), Ella's first day of Princess School is off to a lousy start. Then she meets silly Snow, adventurous Rapunzel, and beautiful, sheltered Rose. Ella's new friends make Princess School bearable—even fun. But can they help Ella stand up to her horrible steps in time for the Coronation Ball?

In stores this May!

PS1T

www.scholastic.com